Berty Ashley is a molecular biologist with the Dystrophy Annihilation Research Trust and works with rare genetic disorders. What is not rare though is to see him conducting quizzes or attending them. He is the author of the popular *Easy Like Sunday Morning* series of quizzes published in *The Hindu*'s *Sunday* magazine. Berty is also a lover of music—not only playing but collecting, as is evident by his growing stack of vinyl records of Jazz, Prog, Hindustani and Heavy metal music. He and his partner, Akhila, live in Bengaluru, surrounded by books, music, and an assortment of pens and guitars.

Akhila Phadnis is a freelance translator. She holds a Masters in Translation Studies from Durham University, UK, and in Psychology from Madras University, Chennai, Tamil Nadu. She enjoys reading, practising calligraphy, learning new languages, quizzing, board games, and taking long walks by the beach.

The Grand HISTORY QUIZ

BERTY ASHLEY
AND
AKHILA PHADNIS

RUPA

Published by
Rupa Publications India Pvt. Ltd 2019
7/16, Ansari Road, Daryaganj
New Delhi 110002

Sales centres:
Allahabad Bengaluru Chennai
Hyderabad Jaipur Kathmandu
Kolkata Mumbai

ISBN: 978-93-5333-590-8

First impression 2019

10 9 8 7 6 5 4 3 2 1

The moral right of the author has been asserted.

CONTENTS

INTRODUCTION

If there's one subject that constantly makes it to the list of the 'most boring subject taught in school', it is history. Children do not realize the importance of learning history until it is no longer in the curriculum. How do we know that? Because that's precisely what happened in Berty's case. In school, he studied history only to ensure he got good grades. If someone had told him then that in the not-too-distant-future he would be actively searching for historical nuggets and facts and that he would share fascinating tidbits from history on WhatsApp, he would have laughed (and been confused as WhatsApp did not exist then). Akhila was always fascinated by history and thought of it, initially, as intriguing and magnificent stories from the past. It's only today that both of us realize to what extent history is also about the present!

Nowadays when we visit a new place, or watch a documentary about a place, we look through all the information available which can give us an idea about where we are and what has transpired over the ages for us to be here! We have come to a point where we find ourselves constantly talking about history—whether of music, books, politics, social events or arts! After all, there are so many magnificent stories and episodes that both guide us and warn us in the present—and help us anticipate the future.

What we have set out to do in this book is to present these magnificent stories and episodes to you, but in a manner which will hopefully pique your interest and encourage you to research more by yourself. If you read these questions, you will realize that they have been peppered with clues and seasoned with extra facts that introduce you to the subject while making it easier for you to answer them. On finding the answer, if you decide to close the book, head to a library or the Internet and search for more details then that would be a mission accomplished for us. Our library at home has its fair share of fiction, comics, fantasy and trivia books. But there is also a separate section on various histories—and one that we are constantly looking to add to. We do not presume to have complete knowledge about any of the themes presented here, nor do we even assume that we have all the best bits from history. We just want to present to you some of our favourite funda and trivia from the annals of history.

A people without the knowledge of their past history, origin and culture is like a tree without roots.

—Marcus Garvey

1. IN THE BEGINNING....

1. This is an archaeological site of the Palaeolithic age which shows the earliest traces of human life on the Indian subcontinent. Found between Nagpur and Bhopal, it was declared a World Heritage Site in 2003. Some of the rock paintings found here are approximately 30,000 years old and there is evidence that Homo erectus inhabited the area more than 100,000 years ago. What is the name of this historic place?

2. It is an oft-quoted fact that a certain large animal was still alive 1,000 years after the Pyramid of Giza was built. Fossils indicate that this mammal lived on all continents except Australia and South America. While most of this species died out about 10,500 years ago (causes cited include climate change and hunting by humans) a small group of them survived on an

island in the Bering Sea until 5000 years ago (after the Pyramid of Giza was built, though they were not in Egypt). This group is now believed to have become extinct due to climate change, where rising sea-levels led to their island home shrinking in size and fresh water being replaced by salt water, eventually leading to their extinction as their drinking water disappeared. What is the name of this magnificent creature?

3. There is evidence that since Neolithic times, there were ancient surgeons who performed 'trepanation', which initially used to have a high mortality rate. The Mayans (1000 CE) standardized and perfected the surgical techniques over time, with fatalities dropping to just 10 per cent. The procedure required the surgeon to make a hole in a particular part of the body, thereby decreasing the pressure inside. This process is still performed, though it is far safer and less dangerous, now that a technique such as the 'orbital transit lobotomy' has been developed. In which part of the body is a hole made during trepanning?

4. Kushim was an accountant from Mesopotamia from around 3200 BCE, and there is a clay tablet which records that over the course of 37 months, he received 29,086 measures of barley. This clay tablet is now part of the The Schøyen Collection. Why is Kushim a special name in the annals of history, apart from being someone who received quite a lot of barley?

5. In 1974, scientists discovered the oldest known human ancestor in Ethiopia. The 3.2-million-year-old skeleton was eventually named 'Lucy'. From the species *Australopithecus afarensis*, her skeleton seems to provide evidence for the argument of human evolution that bipedalism (walking on two legs) preceded increase in brain size. After making the discovery, palaeoanthropologist Donald Johanson headed back to his campsite with his team and, to celebrate, started playing his favourite tape, 'Sgt. Pepper's Lonely Hearts Club Band'. How did our oldest known human ancestor get her name?

6. The *Arachis hypogaea* is a legume crop grown mostly for its edible seeds, which are often considered one of the healthiest foods and has been in use for thousands of years. One very popular use of the seed nowadays is in the form of a paste which can either be crunchy or smooth. The earliest reference to it is found in the Aztec and Incan civilizations where they ground the seeds into a paste. Later in the sixteenth century, people in West Africa also made this paste and ate it with honey, creating a version that is closer to the food we are now familiar with. What item is this that you would most probably use when you need to have a quick breakfast or snack?

7. This time period spans 56 million years and is known as the 'Age of the Reptiles'. Named after a mountain

range in the Western Alps, huge herbivorous dinosaurs roamed the Earth during this period. In popular entertainment, this time is usually shown to be over-run by ferocious carnivores, unfortunately that's all false as these carnivores lived almost a million years after this period. What is the name of this peaceful and really long period?

8. On 12 September 1940, 18-year-old Marcel Ravidat's dog fell into a hole. He rescued the dog and in the process discovered a cave. He returned with three of his friends, hoping to find a secret route to a manor. What they discovered though became a UNESCO World Heritage Site that provided conclusive evidence of human existence in that area from the Upper Palaeolithic time. What they discovered had been perfectly preserved for 17,000 years, but since then had faded and was closed to the public. What did the boys discover, copies of which were later displayed in a museum nearby?

9. Jebel Irhoud is the remnants of a limestone cave in Morocco. In 1960, the area was being mined for baryte when a miner discovered a skull in the wall of the cave. He gave it to an engineer who kept it as a souvenir and eventually gave it to the university. Eventually more skeletons were found and they were thought to be around 40,000 years old, but on radiocarbon dating were dated to be more than 315,000 years old. The

skull, on closer scrutiny, turned out to be a particular species, which they did not realize had been so prolific at that time. This place gave rise to the theory that early humans were spread across the continent. What is the name of this species that was found, whose name in Latin means 'wise man'?

10. The oldest mummies in the world have been discovered in a country far away from Egypt and pre-dating the Egyptian mummies by 2,000 years. These 7,000-year-old mummies are red or black in colour, depending on the method used to prepare the bodies. The country in which they were found has applied for the UNESCO World Heritage status, hoping to draw more attention to and more resources for these mummies, which have been preserved through millennia, thanks to the arid desert soil. What is the name of this country?

ANSWERS

1. Bhimbetka Rock Shelters
2. Woolly mammoth
3. Skull
4. The first named person in history
5. From The Beatles' song 'Lucy in the Sky with Diamonds' on that tape
6. Peanut butter

7. Jurassic

8. The Lascaux Cave paintings

9. Homo sapiens

10. Chile

If you don't know history, then you don't know anything. You are a leaf that doesn't know it is part of a tree.

—Michael Crichton

2. ART AND ARTEFACTS

1. In 2012, archaeologists discovered flutes that were carbon-dated to reveal they were between 42,000 to 43,000 years old, making them the oldest known musical instruments.* These and the previous record-holding flutes, dating back to 40,000 years, would therefore be products of the Palaeolithic age, a time when humans used primarily stone tools. The materials used are bird bones (from vultures) and a certain material that is much in demand even today. In fact, the species from which this material was obtained is now extinct, but traders continue to sell material that may or may not actually belong to the original species. In order to protect certain animals that are poached for the same product today, the Convention on International Trade in Endangered Species of Wild Fauna and Flora (CITES) is proposing to introduce strict regulations

on the trade of this product, in 2019, to protect the related living species today. This would, interestingly, make the original species the first extinct species to be protected by this regulation! What is this product and what is the name of the extinct species?

2. In an exciting art discovery in 2018, archaeologists found a series of paintings of a cow-like creature in a cave named Lubang Jeriji Saléh, located on an island. Dating back to almost 40,000 years, these became the oldest-known figurative cave paintings discovered so far. Interestingly, the previous record-holder for the oldest known figurative cave paintings, (depictions of babirusa or 'pig-deer') was also from the same country, but in another location. What is the name of this country?

3. This being was not initially depicted as a person in Indian art and was, instead, represented through symbols such as an empty throne, a horse without a rider or a depiction of a footprint under a certain tree. The Greek influence on the kingdom of Gandhara led to the first depictions of this being as a person. Who is this being and what is the tree associated with them?

4. Trajan's Column, in Rome; the Bayeux Tapestries in England; the depiction of Napoleon crossing the Alps (among others) are all examples of artwork depicting exaggerated versions of historical events. The veracity

of some of the depictions in the panels of the Bayeux Tapestries, for example, has been questioned. One of the reasons given for this lack of veracity is that all these works were commissioned by or for the victors of these events. A certain word, used to describe these artworks, was used in a similar way in the twentieth century and was chiefly associated with regimes such as the Soviet Union, Mao's China or with communication put out by the American CIA. What is this word?

5. This text lays down guidelines for the creation of Hindu images or sculptures. It specifies the proportions, gestures, postures, etc., that can be used, which explains the homogeneity of Hindu artwork across the centuries. What is the name of this text, derived, unsurprisingly, from the Sanskrit word for sculpture and text?

6. These statues called Moai, created between the late 1000s and the 1600s, have been the subject of much mystery and speculation. They are believed to be the spirits of the chiefs of Rapa Nui, which is the original name of the island where they are found. In 2019, scientists proposed that the Moai and the platforms they were often found on were originally located close to fresh water resources and this could be the answer to part of the mystery surrounding their positioning (though, of course, scientists do not know this definitively yet). However, how they were made

and transported to these sites, given that they were produced by a Stone Age culture, is still unknown, though theories have been proposed. In 1722, a Dutch explorer became the first European visitor to this island, which he named after the day he visited it. This name then went back to Europe and it is how this island is known in many parts of the world today. How are the Rapa Nui island statues collectively known to the world at large today?

7. The Bamiyan valley in Afghanistan is most famous for the monumental statues of the Buddha that it housed, until they were destroyed by the Taliban in 2001. However, another exciting discovery has been made in the caves of the valley—archaeologists discovered paintings on the walls that dated back to the fifth century CE but they were made using a technique that was 'invented' in Europe only centuries later, around the time of the Renaissance. What is this technique that is associated with European Renaissance artists such as Leonardo da Vinci and Raphael?

8. In medieval times, the structure of cathedrals in Europe was transformed by certain architectural designs such as the flying buttress, ribbed vaults in the roofs and pointed arches. Durham Cathedral, in the UK, where construction began in the 1000s, is the first known example of ribbed vaults, while the Chartres Cathedral in France is another famous example of these new

forms of support. The importance of these innovations was that they all eased the burden on load-bearing walls by displacing the weight and forces to external supports or other supports such as pillars and arches.

As a result, a certain element could now be added to these walls which could not be added earlier for fear of weakening the walls. What was this feature that transformed the interior of the building and today, is considered almost synonymous with church or cathedral architecture, especially in Europe?

9. 'Cave 16', as it is sometimes referred to, contains one of the largest rock-carved temples in the world. Hewn out of a single giant rock, this temple dedicated to the Hindu god Shiva features elaborate decorations inside and outside. It was built by the Rashtrakuta dynasty, with construction starting under Raja Dantidurga and continuing for about 150 years. The complex in which this cave is found has caves numbered according to age and theme. Thus, Caves 1-12 are Buddhist creations, carved out between 200 BCE to 600 CE; 13-29 are Hindu temples, built over about 400 years, starting from 500 CE; and caves 30-34 are Jain temples built between 800 and 1000 CE. What are these 34 caves collectively known as?

10. This civilization flourished between 200 BCE and 600 CE in Peru and is famous for huge drawings made

on the surface of the desert there. These drawings have survived for between 500 to 2,000 years thanks to the conditions in the desert (very little wind or rain). The magnitude and detailing of these drawings, called the _____ Lines, could only be truly appreciated from the air. Thus, pilots flying over this area who for the first time, brought these detailed drawings to people's attention. There are many theories to explain these drawings, from theories of communication with aliens to the theory that people used these geoglyphs to communicate with gods by moving along the lines and carrying out rituals for rain and fertility. What is the name of this civilization after whom the lines are named, and which was driven to extinction by a generation-long drought in 5 CE?

11. The Boscoreale Treasure was discovered by accident when some workmen were digging at a known historical site. While waiting for wages, they idly explored further and found a buried vault. One of the workers slipped in, discovered a mound of treasure and hid it from everyone except his employer, who sold the treasure and paid the worker well. Forty-one of these items were bought by the Louvre, with financial aid from the Baron de Rothschild. Today, they constitute one of the finest finds of artefacts from Roman times dating back to around 79 CE, being remarkably well-preserved, thanks to a certain

incident. What was this tragic incident whose result was the near-perfect preservation of an entire site?

12. The shore temples in the south Indian town of Mahabalipuram are renowned for their architecture, and for a legend that states that there were many more of these shore temples, which disappeared later. A certain event in 2004 seemed to reveal the existence of certain ruins, and archaeologists have now carried out explorations that seem to confirm the existence of now-sunken temples. What was this 2004 event that made waves around the world and revealed the existence of these temples?

13. Wassily Kandinsky, the famous Russian artist, was one of the pioneering figures of abstract art. He once attended a concert by a famous musician in 1896, and suddenly realized that music, like art, had no tangible form and yet stirred the emotions. This insight inspired him to create some of his greatest works, which had musical titles such as *Composition*. Which famous musician's work had inspired Kandinsky (his music was also famously used in the *Looney Tunes* show, *A Night at the Opera*)?

14. *The Scream* is a popular 1893 painting by Norwegian artist Edvard Munch. The artist was inspired to create the painting when he went for a walk at sunset and the clouds turned blood-red and he sensed 'an infinite

scream passing through nature.' The painting has become iconic, being referred to multiple times in popular culture over the years. In 2004, two researchers retraced Munch's steps and found the place which they believe inspired him. After studying Munch's journals and investigating the sky phenomena that might have created the blood-red sky, they came to the conclusion that the unique nature of the scenery would have been caused by a dramatic and tragic natural disaster that had taken place on 27 August 1883 on the other side of the world. What catastrophic event was this that caused atmospheric shifts all over the world and inspired this painting?

15. This film, based on the life of a famous artist, was also unique in the way that it was made. It is the first animated feature film in history, made entirely with oil painting, with over 125 oil painters contributing to the frames in the film. What is the name of this film which explored the death of a famous artist and was animated entirely in his style of painting?

ANSWERS

1. Ivory; woolly mammoth
2. Indonesia: Luban Jeriji Saléh is in Borneo. The previously-discovered paintings were on Sulawesi.
3. The Buddha; the Bodhi tree

4. Propaganda

5. *Shilpa shastra*

6. Easter Island statues: The explorer visited the island on Easter Sunday.

7. Oil painting

8. Stained glass windows

9. The Ellora Caves

10. Nazca; the Nazca (or Nasca) Lines

11. The eruption of Mt. Vesuvius and the destruction of Pompeii

12. The 2004 tsunami in the Indian Ocean

13. Richard Wagner

14. The Krakatoa eruption

15. *Loving Vincent*, on Vincent Van Gogh

The most effective way to destroy people is to deny and obliterate their own understanding of their history.

—George Orwell

3. CULTURAL HISTORY

1. The original specimen was destroyed by King Pusyamitra in 2 BCE and its replacement was destroyed by King Shasanka in 7 BCE. The one presently seen at the site was nurtured by the British archaeologist Alexander Cunningham after the previous one died of old age. What is this entity that sheltered a spot from which one of the major Eastern religions started?

2. These were a series of three legendary conferences of which two were supposed to have happened in cities that do not exist anymore as they are thought to have been lost to the sea. The third conference was held during the fourth century BCE in the present-day city of Madurai. These conferences played a significant role in inspiring political, social and literary movements in a classical language. Which language is this and what were these conferences known as?

3. One of the major changes in the Indian Army post-Independence was the dropping of a certain term from their vocabulary. The term is derived from the Persian word for 'soldier' and is, till this day, the term preferred by British historians. Indian historians typically don't use the term and use another word, meaning 'young' instead. Most of us would have first come across this term this term in reference to a certain event that took place in Meerut in 1857. What is the term that the Indian army dropped and what term has replaced it?

4. A particular ethno-religious group has two main subcultures named 'Ashkenazi' and 'Sephardi'. The first word means 'German' and the second means 'Spanish' in a particular language which the group uses as a sacred language. The former refers to those who established communities along the River Rhine in Western Germany and Northern France. The latter refers to those who traditionally resided in Spain and Portugal. Which is this ethno-religious group and which language contains these words?

5. This transformation began in North Britain, spread to Western Europe and within a few decades, to North America. Experts believe that this was the most important event in the history of humanity, after the domestication of animals and fire. The earliest recorded use of this term was in a letter from 6 July 1799 by Frenchman Louis-Guillaume Otto. This sea

change also led to an unprecedented rise in the rate of population growth which has continued to the present day and is implicated in the accelerated rate of global warming. What is the name of this revolution that started sometime in 1760?

6. Scientists and researchers working among the native inhabitants of this land have discovered that their legends and oral histories can accurately track changing sea levels 7,000 to 10,000 years back. This implies that these stories have been accurately passed on through 400 generations! It was earlier believed that unless it was written down, orally transmitted information could only accurately be passed on for about 800 years. These people have inhabited this land for about 65,000 years and were reasonably isolated from the outside world until their land was colonized in the 1780s. Their story-telling method included cross-generational verification, where the stories would be narrated from one generation to another in the presence of the youngest generation and this could explain the high degree of accuracy as the tales were passed down through the years. Which fascinating land do these native inhabitants belong to?

7. Born in present-day Patna in 475 CE, this person is the first mathematician-astronomer from ancient India. His major work covers arithmetic, algebra, plane trigonometry and spherical trigonometry. It also

contains continued fractions, quadratic equations, sums-of-power series and a table of sines. In it he talks about how Pi is irrational, a theory which was only proved in Europe in 1761. He later wrote another book which had descriptions of astronomical instruments and water clocks. The Inter-University Centre for Astronomy and Astrophysics in Pune has a statue of him in its courtyard. Who is this pioneer physicist?

8. Margrethe II is the current Queen of Denmark and has been on the Danish throne for 47 years. She studied prehistoric archaeology at Cambridge, followed by political science at Aarhus University. She is an accomplished painter and once sent some of her illustrations under the pseudonym Ingahild Grathmer to a legendary author. That author was struck by the similarity of her drawings to his own style, so her art was used in the 1977 Danish edition of his magnum opus. Being fluent in Danish and English, she further went on to work as an official translator of the same. Which author and book did Grathmer translate and draw for?

9. This organization was founded in Austria in 1923 and in 1938 came under the control of Nazi Germany and was moved to Berlin. Thereafter, many notable members of the SS served as its president, including Reinhard Heydrich who headed the Gestapo, among other organizations. After the defeat of the Nazis in the

war, the Allies revived the organization with officials from Belgium, France and the UK. To keep itself neutral it does not undertake interventions or activities of a political, military, religious or racial nature and focuses primarily on public safety and transnational crimes. What is the name of this organization?

10. In 1905, an earthquake of 7.8 Richter magnitude hit the district of Kangra in Northeast India, killing thousands and destroying most buildings. Most people moved out of the region and one of the once-prosperous villages there, which was named after an English Lieutenant Governor, was on the verge of becoming a ghost town. In 1960, Nauzer Noworojee, who owned the oldest general store in the town, wrote to the government of India with a proposal to invite a certain person who was searching for a new home. The proposal was eventually taken up and it soon turned the village into the bustling suburb it is now. What is the name of this village which is affectionately known as Little Lhasa' and to whom was the invitation extended by Noworojee?

ANSWERS

1. The Bodhi tree at Bodhgaya

2. Tamil Sangams

3. Sepoy (Persian *sipahi*); jawan

4. Judaism, Hebrew

5. The Industrial Revolution

6. Australia

7. Aryabhatta

8. J.R.R. Tolkien; *The Lord of the Rings*

9. Interpol

10. McLeod Ganj, Dharmshala; The Dalai Lama

Study the past if you would define the future.

—Confucius

4. RULERS

1. This ruler was the son of a Gupta emperor and a Licchavi princess and expanded his kingdom to vast lengths. He is said to have marched the length of the South-Eastern coast of India and at one time ruled an empire that stretched from the River Ravi to the River Brahmaputra and from the Himalayas to Central India. He is supposed to have performed the *Ashvamedha*, in which a horse was sent to wander for a year and if it came back unharmed then all the land it traversed would belong to its master. Who was this emperor whose reign, in the middle of the fourth century CE, went undefeated?

2. This person was an Umayyad general who conquered the Sindh and Punjab regions along the River Indus. His conquest enabled Islamic expansion into India. He is often referred to as the first Pakistani, and

Muhammed Ali Jinnah claimed that the Pakistan movement started when this general put his foot on the soil of Sindh. Who is this general who has a huge port in Karachi named after him?

3. In the Battle of Karnal, the Persians defeated the Mughals just 110 kilometres away from Delhi. The commander of the Persians was one of the most powerful Iranian rulers in the history of the nation and a military genius. He idolized Genghis Khan and Timur and at one time he was West Asia's most powerful sovereign, ruling over what was considered to be the most powerful empire in the world. On his orders, the Persians ransacked the city and plundered the treasury, carrying back with him the Peacock Throne, the Koh-i-Noor and the Darya-ye-Noor diamonds, and leaving 30,000 dead in Delhi. The loot gave him so much wealth that he removed all taxes back home for 3 years. Who is this leader and which Mughal emperor did he defeat?

4. This term refers to an ethnic, cultural or racial group that speaks or spoke languages such as Arabic, Amharic, Tigre, Hebrew, Aramaic, etc. The term was first used in the 1780s, when it was derived from the name of the eldest son of Noah, the character in the Bible who built an ark to save his family and animals from a flood. Abraham, the patriarch of the Hebrews and the Arabs, was one of the descendants of this son

and hence it is only fitting his name is used. What is his name and what is the term used?

5. This person was the heir-apparent to Shah Jahan but lost the throne to his younger brother Muhiuddin, who later had him executed. He was a great patron of the arts and was inclined towards philosophy and mysticism rather than military pursuits. The library of the Delhi archaeological department is named after him as he had commissioned it. There is much debate about how the history of the subcontinent would have changed if he had prevailed over his brother who was a dominant, militaristic ruler. Who is this person and how do we better know his brother who eventually became the last effective Mughal emperor?

6. Although her reign was short-lived, lasting only three-and-a-half years, this queen made history for being a valiant warrior and a strong ruler, bringing stability to her kingdom following her brother's dissolute rule. Her reign was marked by courtiers constantly conspiring to end her rule as they objected to serving a female ruler, as well as religious leaders objecting to her boldness. Who was this fascinating ruler who was the only woman to have ruled as head of the Delhi Sultanate?

7. This king of Mali is today known to be the richest man ever to have lived. He ruled Mali at a time when

the kingdom is estimated to have possessed half the money in the world at the time. He took over the throne when his brother, the king, who was an avid and curious traveller, left on a voyage across the sea from which he never returned. This king made his country and himself famous when he travelled from his kingdom to Mecca across the Sahara and Egypt along with a massive retinue, all dressed in the finest clothing. Stories of his wealth and generosity spread far and wide. He is supposed to have distributed so much gold on his travels that gold prices plummeted in the region for a decade! Who is this king who also invested heavily in the arts and education and whose legacy includes the University of Sankoré, which went on to become one of the greatest centres of learning in the world in the fourteenth century?

8. Maria Letizia Ramolino was born in Corsica and at the age of 13 married a trainee attorney who was 17 at that time. She went on to raise eight children. She is known as the 'Mother of Monarchs' as most of her children went on to become rulers. Some of these children were the eldest son Joseph (King of Spain), Jérôme (King of Westphalia), Louis (King of Holland) and Caroline (Queen of Naples). The most famous of them was the second eldest son who declared himself emperor and was also responsible for installing some of his siblings on various thrones. Who is this son

who took good care of his mother during his exile?

9. This powerful empress started out as a mistress of the emperor. Upon his death, she married his son and when he also died, she took over the throne herself in the late seventh century CE. In order to cement her status as the ruler of her country and to squash criticism of a female ruler, she used myths and legends of powerful women and divinities to back her power. Who is this political genius who was the only woman emperor in the 5,000 years of her country's history? What is the name of this country that she helped to build and maintain, and that is such a powerful force in the world today?

10. Historical reports state that a 'Friends of the Jacobin' club was set up in Mysore in the 1790s. The Jacobins were French radicals who played a major role in the French Revolution to overthrow the monarchy and establish a Republic. It was, therefore, astonishing that the records of the club stated that the Mysore club had been set up by a monarch! Not only that, but that the monarch had called himself Citizen _____ in the Revolutionary style. Historians today argue that these records are fake and were part of British propaganda, aimed at making the ruler look dangerous and an ally of the French (the British and French fought fiercely in India for territories). Who was this powerful ruler

who fought against the British and whose history has been severely distorted?

ANSWERS

1. Samudra Gupta
2. Muhammad bin Qasim
3. Nader Shah; Muhammed Shah
4. Shem; Semitic languages
5. Dara Shukoh; Aurangazeb
6. Razia Sultan (she disliked the title 'Sultana', which was given to consorts and not the rulers)
7. Mansa Musa
8. Napoleon Bonaparte
9. Wu Zhao (or Wu Zetian), Empress of China
10. Tipu Sultan

That men do not learn very much from the lessons of history is the most important of all the lessons that history has to teach.

—Aldous Huxley

5. RULERS AND FAMOUS CITIES

1. This ancient historic city was the capital of the Roman, Byzantine, Latin and Ottoman empires. For about 1,000 years, it was the largest and wealthiest city in all of Europe. The city was deliberately built to rival Rome and was famed for its massive and complex defences. The earliest reference to it is by Pliny the Elder who refers to it as 'Lygos'. It got its present name from a Roman emperor who transferred the capital to this city in 330 CE and called it 'New Rome'. Which historic city is this?

2. This city derived its name from the one given to it by Akbar in 1583. The name is made up of two parts, from the Arabic word for 'Lord' and the Persian word for 'to create a garden'. The city lies close to Triveni Sangam— the confluence of the three rivers Ganga, Yamuna and Sarasvati—which makes it a propitious

place for conducting sacrifices. The original ancient name (and current name) which means 'place of sacrifice or offering' comes from this location of the city. This name was reverted to in 2018. What is the current name and what name did it displace?

3. According Greek historians, in 326 BCE a Paurava king fought this iconic king at the battle of Hydaspes river. He lost the battle and when asked by the triumphant emperor, 'How would you like to be treated?', answered, 'As befits a king.' The triumphant emperor was supposedly impressed by this, and released him and granted him dominion over lands to the south-east. Who were these two historical leaders?

4. Simeon Saxe-Coburg-Gotha became the ruler of his country at the age of six in 1943. He was the last reigning monarch of this country, as he was overthrown by a Communist revolution in 1946 after which he lived in exile with his family until the 1990s, when he returned to his country. In an interesting turn of events, in 2001 he contested and won parliamentary elections to become the democratically elected prime minister of his country for a full term, between 2001 and 2005. In which interesting country did this happen?

5. It is believed that this military leader wrote to Tipu Sultan in 1798, assuring him of his support against the British and sharing his plan to march from his country

to India to help Tipu liberate his land from the British. As it happened, this leader's army was defeated in Egypt and could not make it as far as India. Who is this charismatic and ambitious leader who conquered many lands and helped end a revolution in his own country?

6. This king suffered from chronic bronchitis and was close to death. His chief physician knew that the end was near but realized that if the king passed away after midnight, the news would not be printed in the respected morning papers but in the less respected evening journals, an embarrassment for the family and also an affront to the king's dignity. Thus, to hasten the process the king was injected with morphine and cocaine after which he passed away at 11:55 p.m. and news of the death made it to the morning papers. Who is this king, who was the first monarch of the House of Windsor?

7. The Greek king Mithridates VI of Pontus ruled from about 120–63 BCE. His father Mithridates V was poisoned by unknown persons at a lavish banquet and he died. Mithridates VI went on to expand the Pontus kingdom but was eventually defeated by Pompey. Not wanting to face the public, he attempted suicide and got his daughters to do the same. They died but he failed because of something he had kept doing throughout his life as a precautionary measure. How

did he attempt suicide and what was the precautionary measure he took?

8. This Belgian king set up a private fiefdom in Central Africa, which he called the _____ Free State. This State, owned by the king, rather than by the Belgian government, witnessed horrific brutalities and exploitation of the local labour. When the mass deaths and barbaric treatment of the people became a topic of international criticism, the Belgian government took over the territory and the administration of the region. Rather than being publicly addressed, the atrocities were further hushed up for many years, leading to sharp criticism today of the racist and callous attitudes displayed by all parties involved. Who was this brutal ruler and what was the name of this country that he set up?

9. This mighty emperor, who became famous for a title meaning 'Universal Ruler', conquered multiple countries and ruled over the largest contiguous empire ever known. Born Temujin, he grew up in hardship and poverty, when his family was abandoned by their clan following his father's death. From these humble beginnings, he fought to make a name for himself, eventually consolidating his hold over all the clans in the region. He then embarked on his military campaigns, going further and further afield. Accounts of his campaigns speak of the terror and horror with

which he and his soldiers were regarded. Who is this emperor?

10. This conqueror was renowned as a military tactician whose warfare killed some 17 million people (5 per cent of the world's population at the time) and he ruled over much of Asia in the fourteenth century CE. In 1405, he died during a winter campaign. His body was embalmed with musk and rose water, wrapped in linen, laid in an ebony coffin and sent to Samarkand, where it was buried. In 1941, Josef Stalin sent a team of archaeologists to open the coffin and they allegedly discovered an inscription saying: 'Whoever opens my tomb shall unleash an invader more terrible than I.' They went ahead and opened it. Two days later, Hitler invaded Russia, ignoring Germany and Russia's mutual non-aggression treaty and leading to the eventual death of 26 million people. A year later, the conqueror's body was claimed to have been re-buried as per Islamic tradition and shortly thereafter, the German forces surrendered and retreated from their fruitless quest to conquer Russia. Whose remains did Stalin exhume?

ANSWERS

1. Constantinople
2. Prayagraj, Allahabad

3. Alexander and Porus

4. Bulgaria

5. Napoleon Bonaparte of France

6. George V

7. He drank poison but had been drinking small amounts throughout his life, to build immunity against an attempt similar to what had happened to his father.

8. Leopold II; the Congo Free State

9. Gengis Khan

10. Taimur Lang or Tamerlane

If history were taught in the form of stories, it would never be forgotten.

—Rudyard Kipling

6. HISTORY MYSTERY

1. The North African elephant is thought to be a possible subspecies of the African bush elephant or possibly a separate species by itself that existed in North Africa. It went extinct in ancient Roman times and was thought to be more tameable than its southern cousin, which were too wild to be tamed. There is no verifiable literature about these animals and the only proper account of them is from an iconic event in history in which they played a major part. Scholars think that these elephants might have been the ones that helped a certain military commander take a never-before-tried route in his campaign to defeat the Romans. Which historical event are these now-forgotten pachyderms supposed to have played a major role in?

2. There are various theories that try to explain why an important part of an ancient and famous monument

went missing. While it was once popularly believed that this was caused by Napoleon's army firing a cannonball and damaging this monument, paintings and drawings of the monument that predate Napoleon also show a missing part. It is now believed that this goes further back, and one popular theory is that of an Arab scholar from the fifteenth century, who attributes it to Muhammad Sa'im al-Dahr, who in 1378 CE was outraged at local peasants—who were making offerings in order to increase their harvest—and carried out this act of vandalism, leading to him being hanged. Other theories attribute this to British troops, the Mamluks, magic carpets and even, in an iconic comic series, an overweight Frenchman. Which sculpture, dated to 2550 BCE, is at the centre of this mystery? And what is the mysteriously missing part?

3. In 587 BCE, a Babylonian army, under King Nebuchadnezzar II, conquered Jerusalem, sacking the city and destroying the First Temple, a building used by the Jewish people to worship god. The First Temple was supposed to have contained a particular entity that was one of the holiest relics of all time. Ancient sources indicate that the item was either carried back to Babylon or hidden before the city was captured. It is also possible that it was destroyed during the siege. Its location is unknown but many people believe that it is currently in a divinely hidden location in Ethiopia and

will only be revealed when the Messiah appears. Many explorers have spent their lives looking for this and it even features in the most popular fictional account of Indiana Jones. What entity is this and what is it believed to contain?

4. Many ancient writers describe this fantastic construction in what is now modern-day Iraq, with many of them proclaiming it a 'Wonder of the World'. One of the clearest accounts of this structure is by Philo of Byzantium who wrote about it in 250 BCE. Unfortunately, archaeologists have been unable to find any trace of such a construction ever existing. In 2013, a researcher from Oxford hypothesized that perhaps this structure was actually in Nineveh and not where everyone thought it was. Both these cities have unfortunately been ravaged by centuries of war and looting, so it seems unlikely that this mystery will ever be solved. What supposedly beautiful construction is this?

5. In 2019, a new research paper was published, which revived a theory that DNA testing carried out on the shawl of a murder victim had revealed the identity of a famous historical villain, proving it was a Polish barber, whose name had featured among possible suspects at the time of the crime. However, many historians have strongly objected to these findings on many grounds, including the fact that there is no conclusive proof

that the shawl really belonged to the victim, or that the shawl had been free of contamination for the many decades (almost a century) that it had been stored. Name this elusive murder in a case where suspects have included one of Queen Victoria's grandsons, one of her royal physicians and even (a theory posited in the 1990s by writer Richard Wallace) Lewis Carroll!

6. In the late 1870s, the architect of the Loretto Chapel in Santa Fe, New Mexico, died unexpectedly during construction, and the builders later realized that no staircase had been planned for the choir loft. A standard staircase would not work as the chapel was too small. The carpenters were at a loss as to how to create a staircase in such a small space. The nuns at the church prayed for nine days straight and on the tenth day a strange man with just a saw, a square and some wood showed up. He asked for complete privacy and after three months of working behind closed doors, he mysteriously disappeared without anyone knowing who he was. The finished product was a bewitching helical staircase that rose 22 feet, spiralling around twice, but built without any nails. What seemed to be miraculous was the absence of a central column to bear the weight of the people, something which seemed to defy physics. The seemingly free-standing helical staircase is also made of a wood not found in the area. Believing this to be a miracle, who do the

nuns believe was the carpenter, someone who also happens to be the patron saint of Carpentry?

7. During an attempt to circumnavigate the globe in 1937, this person disappeared over the central Pacific Ocean near Howland Island after sending a radio transmission. The official version states that the pilot ran out of fuel and crashed into sea. However, numerous speculations have ranged, from being captured by Japanese forces to hiding and living successfully as a spy for the CIA. Who is this pilot whose life and disappearance is still a matter of debate for those in the field of aviation?

8. This is an illustrated manuscript written in an entirely unknown language. It is named after a bookseller who purchased it in 1912. Radiocarbon dating shows it to have been created in the fifteenth or sixteenth CE. It contains detailed drawings of plants, herbs, stars, zodiac symbols and even has a pharmaceutical section. However, not only is the language unknown, but the plant species drawn in this manuscript are also unknown! Numerous scholars, linguists and cryptologists have attempted to decode the script but have yet to succeed. Researchers are now trying to work with AI to decode the book. What is the name of this mysterious manuscript, which one can see in the Beinecke Rare Book and Manuscript Library at Yale University?

9. In July 1518, a woman in Strasbourg suddenly started doing something in the middle of the street and continued to do so for six days. She was soon joined by others, all doing the same thing, uncontrollably. Within a month, 400 people were performing the same activity in the city and would not stop; many died from a heart attack, stroke or exhaustion. This was called the '_____' Plague of 1518, and many theories were postulated as to the cause behind it. Physicians at that time believed it to be a natural disease caused by 'hot blood'. There is a theory that it could have been mass hysteria, an act to please divine powers or it could have been stress-induced psychosis. The latest theory is that it was caused by food poisoning, because of a psychoactive fungi that might have got into the bread. However, with no clear answer, mystery still surrounds this unique incident in history. What activity did these people die of, that you'd probably have only happy memories of?

10. This great civilization existed between 2500 BCE to 1700 BCE and was larger than the ancient Egyptian and the Mesopotamian civilizations combined. The site of this civilization was identified only in 1921 and designated a UNESCO World Heritage Site in 1980. The secrets behind the identity of the people and their puzzling 4000-year-old pictographic script are yet to be discovered. The people used irrigated

agriculture with sufficient skill to reap the advantages of the spacious and fertile river valley they inhabited, while controlling the formidable annual flood that simultaneously fertilizes and destroys. Mysteriously, all the major sites of this civilization went into sudden decline and disappeared more or less simultaneously. What is the name of this civilization that gets its name from the river it was built around?

11. Built between 4,000 and 5,000 years ago, this was likely a part of a complex of ritualistic structures, including ancient burial mounds and processional routes. The material used to build this was brought from places as far as 160 kilometres away, though it is not known what mode of transport was used. The purpose of this structure is a matter of debate. It is speculated that it could have been used as a cemetery or a ceremonial location for the coronation of Danish kings. Some researchers believe it to be an astrological calendar to follow the lunar and solar months. Some even think it was constructed by ancient alien visitors. When in 1880, there was concern that the structures were sinking into the soil, Charles Darwin investigated and concluded that the culprits were earthworms. What iconic and enigmatic structures are these?

12. Found in Qumran in 1952, this artefact was different from another highly exciting find made here in 1947 by a Bedouin. These earlier finds were manuscripts that

were 2,000 years old, written on papyrus. This new find, however, was made of a different material. The writing on it describes hiding places for vast amounts of gold and valuables, though archaeologists are not sure whether these really exist. What is this mysterious find, named after the material the writing is etched upon?

13. While the existence of this land has been the subject of many myths in recent times, it seems quite certain that it was originally simply invented by the Greek philosopher Plato to serve as an allegory for moral corruption in a society that focused only on material and technological advancement. It was not until 1882, in a former US Congressman's book, _____: *The Antediluvian World* that this land came to be identified as a lost civilization that symbolized the pinnacle of human achievement (which was actually in contrast to Plato's view of the land). What is the name of this mythical land that is today the subject of several films and works of fiction, and was once used by race supremacist and Nazi thinkers to try and prove that the Aryan race was descended from this fabled super-race?

14. This ruler's death is shrouded in mystery. Having conquered vast tracts of lands from Eastern Europe to modern-day Pakistan, he died in Greece at the age of 32. Proposed causes include typhoid, malaria,

poisoning or murder. Contemporary accounts added to the mystery by stating that his body showed no signs of decomposition for six days after his death. In 2019, a researcher from New Zealand suggested that the real cause of death may have been Guillain-Barré Syndrome, an autoimmune disorder whose symptoms match those exhibited by the ruler. Further, since he may have been paralyzed, the king may have died a few days later than suspected, which is why his body showed no immediate sign of decomposition. Who is this legend whose early (and still mysterious) death resulted in him naming no heir and his kingdom breaking up soon after?

15. This person was the first to reach the South Pole as well as the North Pole—each a remarkable achievement in itself! He was also the first man to reach the North Pole by flight. A few years after he made history by reaching the North Pole, this explorer disappeared. He was on a flight searching for fellow explorer Umberto Nobile and was never heard from again. It is assumed that his flight got lost in the fog and crashed, though no wreckage has been found. Who is this truly intrepid explorer?

ANSWERS

1. Hannibal crossing the Alps

2. The Sphinx; the missing nose of the Sphinx

3. The Ark of the Covenant, which contained the Ten Commandments

4. The Hanging Gardens of Babylon

5. Jack the Ripper

6. St. John

7. Amelia Earhart

8. The Voynich Manuscript

9. Dancing

10. Indus Valley Civilization

11. Stonehenge

12. Copper Scroll

13. Atlantis

14. Alexander the Great

15. Roald Amundsen

One cannot and must not try to erase the past merely because it does not fit the present.

—Golda Meir

7. BATTLES GALORE

1. In war if a city is on the verge of being captured, the controlling entity will declare the city as an 'X' city, which indicates that they have abandoned all defensive efforts. The other army will then stop all attacks and simply march in. This is done to protect the historic landmarks and the civilians inside from unnecessary damage. What is 'X', which happened most famously in Rome on 14 August, 1943?

2. The army of this powerful empire attacked Vienna in 1529, as it expanded westward. However, multiple factors, including the Danube, that prevented access to the city from one side, and the weather, which slowed the invading army, allowed the Viennese to prepare to defend themselves even as their allies withdrew. Despite multiple attempts, the invaders failed to seize Vienna and returned to their capital. While

their empire continued to expand, it only expanded towards the East after this and never got further west than Hungary. Which dominant empire was this?

3. Pavlov's House is today a famous monument in this city. This marks the spot where one of the greatest battles of the Second World War was fought. Sergeant Pavlov's platoon captured this house, ejecting the Nazis from it. In doing so, Pavlov lost most of his men and only four survived. There were also ten civilians hiding in the building. For the next two months, Pavlov's surviving men and these civilians, reinforced by only 25 more soldiers, held this single building and prevented the Nazis from advancing. The Germans lost more men trying to take this one apartment building from these 35 people than they did in the entire conquest of Paris! In which famous battle (named after the city) did Pavlov and his platoon play a key role?

4. In 1597, an estimated 300 Japanese ships bore down on Myeongnyang, poised to invade and control the peninsular region. However, one brave admiral refused to give up and told his ruler, 'I still have 12 ships.' He then proceeded to distribute his forces and trap the Japanese in the treacherous waters of the Myeongnyang Strait. His glorious victory against all odds is only one among more than 20 naval victories he oversaw. Which country's navy was lucky enough to count Admiral Yi among its forces?

5. Jean Bernadotte was a French soldier who proved to be an able military commander under the leadership of Napoleon. When his army won a battle in Lübeck, he treated a certain country's soldiers with courtesy and allowed them to return to their home country, where they spread the news of Bernadotte's fairness in maintaining order. Four years later, the monarch of that country was dying with no heir, and they decided to offer the throne to Bernadotte. Eventually in 1810, he was adopted by the monarch and was made the crown prince. After leading the army to many victories, on the monarch's death in 1818, he became king and reigned as King Charles XIV, and his house is on the throne till this day. Which country did this Frenchman become king of, thanks to his being a good person during a war?

6. Norse warriors fought in a nearly uncontrollable, trance-like fury. It has been suggested that the warriors consumed hallucinogens before battles. These warriors were ruthless and murdered at will and destroyed entire communities. They get their name from the fact that they were supposed to have worn the pelt of wild animals when going into battle, or it could be from the fact that they fought bare bodied. It is from their name that we derive a word in the English language, which means 'out of control with anger or excitement; wild or frenzied'. What were the names of these warriors

and what is the word we get from them?

7. Marwari warhorses were bred by Rajput clans by combining the most useful characteristics of Arabians, Turkumans and local stock. The intelligent, fearless and hardy breed was bred to withstand the crippling desert heat and used to fight enemies who had a particular powerful weapon. To tackle these weapons, the Rajputs exploited their weak point and could get up close in battle by attaching long grey tubes to the mouths of the horses. This ensured that they were not attacked by the enemy's biggest weapon. What was that weapon and what were the horses dressed up as?

8. In the Battle of Pelusium in 525 BCE, King Cambyses II of Persia used these unusual 'war' animals to invade Egypt. Knowing that they held a high place in Egyptian society, the king brought hundreds of them into his front lines. As a result, Egyptian archers refused to fire, fearing that they would injure the animals. This led to the first Persian conquest of Egypt. What is this animal that helped the Persians win a battle, but is usually content to just sit on a wall and watch the world go by?

9. The Battle of Marignano was fought between France and the Old Swiss Confederacy between 1494 and 1559. The French had some of the best armoured lancers and artillery in the world and the Swiss brought pikes and

spears. The Swiss lost and found themselves having to fight with the French. When the Congress of Vienna met in 1814–15 to sort out European peace after the French Revolutionary War, the Swiss decided to make a stand and put forth an elegant win-win solution for the whole continent. What did the Swiss decide that holds true till this day?

10. El Salvador and Honduras had always had tension between them, and in 1969, something happened that sparked a war that lasted for a week and killed more than 5,000 people. Although both countries had many issues between them, the war started because of three incidents, which had to happen so that either one of the countries could be represented at a global event that was to take place the following year (1970) in Mexico. The first event ended in favour of Honduras and was followed by riots; the second event ended in favour of El Salvador and was also followed by riots. The third decider event ended in favour of El Salvador, and the very same day, war was declared. It was finally ended through international arbitration. The war is notable for being the last one fought with propeller-driven planes. The war gets its name from the event which instigated the events. What is the name of the war, which sounds more like the name of a video game?

ANSWERS

1. Open City
2. The Ottoman Empire
3. The Battle of Stalingrad (today, Volgograd)
4. Korea
5. Sweden
6. Berserkers; 'going berserk'
7. The enemies used Elephants, and the Rajputs dressed up their horses as baby Elephants (with hoses) that dissuaded the adult elephants from attacking them.
8. Cats
9. To stay neutral in conflicts
10. Football or Soccer War

Somehow the past is a safe place to explore our collective cultural neuroses.

—Tom Hiddleston

8. HISTORICAL BLUNDERS

1. The book *Black Beauty* describes a very famous battle from the point of view of horses, many of which died in the doomed manoeuvre undertaken by the army. What famous blunder was this where, despite having a famous poem celebrating the battle, only 113 (not 600) men died, but 332 horses were killed?

2. In 1958, Chairman Mao of China ordered people to kill animals identified as pests. One particular animal was identified as a pest, and the government believed that killing it would reduce the amount of grain lost. Thus, citizens hunted it, killed its eggs and young and chased them away with loud noises wherever they saw them. Within two years, these animals were driven nearly to extinction. And as a direct result, with their natural predators gone, hordes of insects descended on China and destroyed crops, resulting in a massive

famine. What meek little animal was this, whose disappearance nearly destroyed a country?

3. In a bid to protect a famous mural by Leonardo da Vinci, a curtain was hung up in front of it. Ironically, the curtain ended up causing more damage than good: every time it was drawn or pulled shut, its rings scratched the wall, and when closed it allowed moisture to build up, which had a detrimental effect on the painting. What is the name of this painting that suffered from a surfeit of good intentions?

4. This famous conqueror was badly defeated in Russia (despite managing to get to Moscow), not as much by the Russian army as by the Russian winter, which decimated his forces. Close to 150 years later, another leader invaded Russia, certain of victory. This leader was known to have studied the other conqueror's campaigns and yet failed to take into account this simple natural phenomenon. The Russian army and people resisted for months, until winter set in. The invading army was woefully underprepared for the weather and had also wasted military resources on smaller targets, allowing the Russians to overwhelm them (though not without a tragically huge number of lives lost in Russia). Who was the first conqueror and who was the second, widely considered the greatest villain in living memory?

5. The original recording of this famous historical event exists in the organization that was responsible for it! In 2006, this organization admitted that they had lost the original recordings. In 2009, they released digitally remastered recordings using news footage and recordings from other sources. The mystery of the missing tapes was also solved when it was discovered that these tapes were part of 200 tapes whose contents were erased so that the tapes could be reused, to save money! What giant leap for mankind was this, copies of the recordings of which, thankfully, do exist in abundance from many other sources that broadcast them live on the day it happened?

6. An entirely devastating episode of human history may be the result of an inaccurate translation. When the premier of a certain country was asked about whether they would heed the warnings from their enemies and surrender, he responded with *mokusatsu*, which could mean no comment but could also mean contemptuously dismissing something. Unfortunately, translators chose to translate this as the leader 'contemptuously ignoring' the warnings and this is believed to have contributed to a terrible decision made by an American president. Which country did the commander belong to and what was the decision?

7. A sailor called David Blair was reassigned from one ship to another at the last moment. He was deemed

not experienced enough for this 'magnificent ship.' He departed, disappointed, and in his haste, he accidentally carried away a key to a locker which contained a pair of binoculars. The man who would have used it, Fred Fleet, later said that if he had had the binoculars, he would have seen something earlier and averted the disaster of 15 April 1912, although the accuracy of this is doubted given that the incident took place at night. What would the locked binoculars perhaps have spotted?

8. In 2001, Damien Hirst set up an installation in a West London art gallery, using leftover rubbish from a party. However, when the time came to open the installation to the public, the artist and assistants had to scramble around to recreate the installation. What had happened to it?

9. In the twelfth century CE, a certain rock was discovered near the town of Bleking, in Sweden. It was believed to be covered in mysterious runes. A Danish king's delegation in the 1100s failed to decipher the runes and contemporary records said that they had been worn away. For over 700 years, the rock was believed to be covered in mysterious, ancient runes. Then in 1833, a delegation of the Royal Society of Sciences in Copenhagen identified them as runes and one of their members finally deciphered them partly and translated the runes as a poem or invocation referring

to the great Danish king Harald Wartooth. A Swedish scientist, Worsae Berzellius, heard of this and went to investigate himself. He studied the rock and came up with the one conclusion that no one had before. His view has, since, prevailed. What was Berzellius' answer to a centuries-old mystery?

10. This person was the First Lord of the Admiralty in 1911 (although he is better known in history for later holding the highest governmental post in his country). During the First World War, he planned an amphibious assault against the Ottoman Empire, which he believed would allow the British to join their Russian Allies. This would put pressure on Germany's eastern front and might even tip the balance of the entire conflict. However, he made the mistake of severely underestimating his foes. When the Allied battleships entered the narrow strait, the Ottoman fire sank three of them and severely damaged three others. The Allies failed to gain any ground during the many months of fighting in the Gallipoli Peninsula (indeed, it was considered one of the biggest Allied failures in the war) and this person lost their post because of his failure. Who was this person whose blunder resulted from hubris?

ANSWERS

1. 'The Charge of the Light Brigade', in the Battle of Balaclava

2. The sparrow

3. *The Last Supper*

4. Napoleon; Hitler

5. The Moon landing; the organization is NASA

6. Japan; the use of the atomic bomb

7. The iceberg that hit and sank the Titanic.

8. The rubbish had been cleared up by a member of the cleaning staff who thought it was simply trash lying around after a party.

9. The marks in the rock were no writing at all but simply natural fissures or cracks.

10. Winston Churchill

History isn't about dates and places and wars. It's about the people who fill the spaces between them.

—Jodi Picoult

9. INTREPID AND INNOVATIVE INDIVIDUALS

1. During the reign of King Harshavardhana, a Buddhist monk from India visited India to learn about the country and its culture. This came about reportedly because of a dream he had in 627 CE, which convinced him to journey to India. To achieve this, he had to slip out of the empire unnoticed, travel across the Gobi Desert, escape robbers, travel through modern day Afghanistan and finally reach India. He was known for his extensive translations of Indian Buddhist texts into Chinese, and in his honour, a statue of him was built at the Giant Wild Goose Pagoda which holds all the figurines he had brought with him from India. Who is this intrepid traveller monk?

2. This gentleman was one of the first generation of Indians to receive an university education and went

on to become the president of the Indian National Congress. In 1905, he established an organization to further the cause of Indian education, which organized mobile libraries, founded schools and provided night classes for factory workers. Unfortunately, this organisation is pretty much defunct now. Who was this learned gentleman and what organization did he set up?

3. Manfred von Richthofen was a German fighter pilot with the Deutsche Luftstreitkräfte (Imperial German Air Service) during the First World War. He flew with the fighter wing unit Jagdgeschwader 1, known as 'The Flying Circus' because of how it was transferred from one area of Allied air activity to another. Richthofen is considered to be the ace-of-aces for having single-handedly won 80 air combat battles. Richthofen was a 'Free Lord', which was a title of nobility given to his family. He also had the habit of painting his aircraft red in colour. These two facts let to him being given a nickname by which he became famous the world over. He has been featured in various films, books and even cartoons. In the comic strip *Peanuts*, Snoopy daydreams of flying as a fighter pilot but keeps getting shot down by this character who shares his name with Richthofen. What is Richthofen's nickname?

4. One 21 November 1783, army officer Marquis d'Arlandes and physicist Pilatre de Rozier became the

first two recorded humans in free flight when they took off from the garden of the Château de la Muette, and 25 minutes later, landed in the outskirts of Paris. This historic moment was witnessed by, amongst thousands of citizens, King Louis XVI and a certain Benjamin Franklin from America. Earlier, the king had decided that two criminals would be given this dangerous mission, but Rozier persuaded the king to allow him and d'Arlandes to do it instead. What was the means of transport which allowed them to do this historic excursion?

5. Gertrude Bell was the first graduate in History from Oxford and was a self-taught archaeologist. When she worked in Cairo, she became an influential diplomat, one who could be trusted by the Arabs, so much so that she was given the nickname 'Khatun' which means 'fine lady'. After the Ottoman Empire was dismantled in 1919, Bell, thanks to her familiarity with the tribes in a particular area, was assigned to conduct an analysis. This led to her playing a major role in the creation of a country, which has been at the centre of many controversial decisions over the years. Which country did Bell help establish?

6. This lady, along with her mother and sister, fought for women's right to vote. However, she was considered too left-wing by her organization and was expelled, resulting in her setting up the East London Federation

of Suffragettes. She believed that the Women's Social and Political Union, in which her mother and sister played leading roles, engaged in too much violence. She was a staunch pacifist, enraging several of her family and friends by condemning the violence of the First World War. She approved of the Russian Revolution and personally met (and argued with) Lenin. The British government used her pro-Communist writings to send her to jail for sedition for five months. She moved to Ethiopia towards the end of her life, setting up a Social Service Society and was given a state funeral in Ethiopia upon her death, with the emperor himself attending it. Who is this dynamic and free-spirited woman?

7. Nansen was a Norwegian explorer, scientist and diplomat. He was the first to cross Greenland and his innovations about techniques and equipment revolutionized polar expeditions. He joined the League of Nations in 1921, where he was behind what became known as the 'Nansen Passport'. The First World War had just ended and had created huge turmoil for certain people. Nansen Passports were given to about half a million of these people and 52 countries honoured it. Who were these people covered by the Nansen Passport?

8. This brilliant engineer from Mysore was also a scholar, statesman and the Diwan of Mysore. He designed a

flood protection system for Hyderabad and, at one time, supervised the construction of the biggest dam in Asia. During his service with the princely state of Mysore, he was responsible for founding, among other things, Mysore Soap Factory, Mysore Iron and Steel Works, Bangalore Agricultural University, State Bank of Mysore and the Century Club. A Knight Commander of the British Indian Empire, he established universities and laboratories that are still in operation today. Who is this genius whose birthday is celebrated in India as Engineer's Day?

9. On 1 December 1955, an African-American seamstress got into a bus after a long day's work and sat in the section for 'coloured' people. When the 'white' section filled up, the driver moved the sign and asked her to give up her seat. She refused to and was arrested for that. This led to a boycott of public transport by African-Americans and the formation of an association where a hitherto unknown minister called Martin Luther King Jr. was elected president. This is regarded as a cornerstone of the civil rights moment in the US. Who was the lady who resolutely parked herself in her seat?

10. Queen Liliuokalani (1838–1917) was the first queen and the last sovereign of the Kamehameha dynasty which ruled an archipelago in the Pacific Ocean. She re-drafted the kingdom's constitution and resolutely withstood the Western world's plans to take over her

kingdom. She is also the author of the most famous song from her culture 'Aloha 'Oe'. She was eventually overthrown by soldiers from a country that took over these islands as one of its states. Which archipelago did she rule over?

ANSWERS

1. Xuanzang or Hiuen Tsang
2. Gopal Krishna Gokhale; Servants of India Society
3. The Red Baron
4. Hot air balloon
5. Iraq
6. Sylvia Pankhurst
7. Refugees
8. M. Visvesvaraya
9. Rosa Parks
10. Hawaii

Those who understand history are condemned to watch other idiots repeat it.

—Peter Lamborn Wilson

10. DEMOCRACY AROUND THE WORLD

1. The world's oldest republic existed in the Kathmandu Valley from 400 CE to 750 CE, where it was ruled by a maharaja who was aided by a prime minister in charge of the military and of other ministers. For a few years, a prime minister was actually on the throne and local administration was carried out by village heads or leading families. What was this republic, chiefly made up of the Licchavi clan?

2. This document was inspired by the writings of Rousseau, Voltaire and by texts from other countries, including the Virginia Declaration of Rights, adopted after the American Revolution in 1776. It advocated, among other things, freedom of speech and religion, and guaranteed the equality of all individuals before law. It was drafted by Marquis de Lafayette, with the

help of Thomas Jefferson and was adopted by the newly formed National Assembly of this country two years before it became the preamble of its Constitution. What is the name of this country and what is this historic document?

3. In the early 1960s, the then Tamil Nadu Chief Minister K. Kamaraj was visiting a town in Tirunelveli district. Near a train intersection when he was waiting for the train to cross, he noticed a boy herding cattle and asked him why he was not in school. The boy's reply led to him starting one of the largest programmes of its kind in the world, which has covered more than 115 million children. What is the name of this scheme?

4. This country was guided into democracy by their fourth king. He began the process of setting up a democratic constitution for the country and abdicated in favour of his son in order to allow his son to learn his duties before the next general elections in his country. Today, this kingdom is regarded as a beacon of hope for other nations—it grades its development based on how happy its people are and it is a carbon-negative country, one of a handful in the world to achieve this. What happy, healthy country is this, which, although it is still headed by a king, moves closer to the image of an ideal democracy every year?

5. K.F. Rustamji was a police officer who served as

the chief security officer for Jawaharlal Nehru and eventually played a prominent role in setting up the Border Security Force. In 1978, he visited the jails in Bihar and wrote two articles in *The Indian Express* about the conditions of the undertrials, languishing in the jails for long periods of time, without trials. A lawyer, Kapila Hingoran, read the articles and filed a particular type of petition for the first ever time in India, leading to the release of 40,000 undertrials all over India. What are these petitions called, which led to a revolution in the Indian legal system?

6. In 1159 BCE, Ramesses III wanted to celebrate his thirtieth year on the throne, so plans were set in motion for a grand jubilee in Egypt. Unfortunately, the monthly wages of the tomb-builders and artisans at Set-Ma'at arrived almost a month late, and a scribe had to negotiate with local officials for distribution of corn to the workers. The same issue came up during the next pay cycle, and this time, the workers waited for 18 days beyond their payday and then refused to wait any longer. They put down their tools and marched towards the city shouting, 'We are hungry!' continuing till eventually all dues were settled. What is this the first recorded instance of in the world?

7. When M.K. Gandhi led a mass burning of Indian registration cards in South Africa, it was compared to this event, which took place on 16 December 1773.

A group of demonstrators, some of them dressed as Native Americans, surrounded the *Dartmouth*, which was a ship carrying a certain commodity 'X' shipped by a trading company 'Y'. The demonstrators were protesting a certain law that allowed the company to sell this commodity without paying tax. They boarded the ship, which was anchored in Massachusetts Bay, and threw the cargo overboard. The British government responded harshly and the episode escalated into the American Revolution. The popular name for this episode comes from the place it happened and the commodity that was trashed. What is this episode called and which trading company was its target?

8. This English word comes from a Latin root which means 'white or pure', and Romans seeking to be elected to the senate used to wear white robes signifying their 'honesty'. Till date, our parliamentarians follow the same principle (of wearing white that is, not necessarily honesty). What word used in election terminology arises from the same?

9. This historical leader was kicked out of university in the 1940s for organizing a student strike and was designated a terrorist when he advocated armed resistance to end Apartheid in his country. He was jailed in 1963, as head of the African National Congress—at that time a banned organization fighting apartheid. He was considered a communist by the United States

of America and, indeed, it was only in 2008 that the US removed his name from a terrorism watchlist, a fact that might have shocked the world given that this person was now an acknowledged hero and bringer of peace. Who is this iconic rebel and leader?

10. The first elections in India, in 1951, were held in 68 phases or stages. In fact, the very first phase was held in a region then called Chini Tehsil, which had to vote in October as it was feared that later in the year heavy snow would cut off the region and make it inaccessible. Thirty-two-year-old Shyam Saran Negi has the distinction of being the first voter of Independent India to vote in an election in the country! What state did he belong to, which also had the distinction of being the first state in India to ever go to polls?

ANSWERS

1. Vaishali

2. France; The Rights of Man and the Citizen

3. The midday meal scheme

4. Bhutan

5. Public Interest Litigation

6. A worker's strike

7. Boston Tea Party; the East India Company

8. Candidate (from 'candidum')

9. Nelson Mandela

10. Himachal Pradesh

History is a guide to navigation in perilous times. History is who we are and why we are the way we are.

—David McCullough

ACKNOWLEDGEMENTS

The authors would like to thank their parents and grandparents for ensuring that their lives were filled with history books, and for telling stories and sharing anecdotes. Berty's interest in Indian history started when his grandmother told him that she had been standing in the middle of the American College Hall when she heard Jawaharlal Nehru's 'Tryst with Destiny' speech on the radio on 15 August 1947. Akhila would like to thank her parents, in particular, for quoting from history and encouraging her to dig deeper whenever she encountered a new fact or anecdote.

Both the authors would like to thank their teachers from school for instilling in them a respect for the past at an early age. Akhila would like to thank all the staff at B.A.S.S. and Kalakshetra for helping the students look ahead to the future while acknowledging a highly syncretic tradition.

Finally, they would also like to acknowledge their joint love for Terry Deary for his absolutely adorable, excellently engaging and fantastically funny *Horrible Histories* series. There has always been a separate shelf in the library for his books in all of the places they have ever lived in. Berty would like to put on record his gratitude to Abhilash Sethurayer, Abhijeet Shyam and Pragadeesh Meenakumar for always looking out for more HH books and sharing random facts from history every now and then.